I0624612

Praise for *The Reckoning*

"A thought provoking, challenging and ultimately inspiring portrait of the judgement seat of Christ. Written by a theologian with a deep command of the Scriptural depiction of the Kingdom of God and the world to come, Dr Lee paints a portrait [that is] saturated by the shocking grace and goodness of God to us in Christ.

"Short and eminently accessible to any reader [*The Reckoning*] vivifies these truths by envisaging this experience for an individual believer and a number of his contemporaries in whom most of us will hear echoes of our own shortcomings and struggles.

"The end result challenges our assumptions and beautifully reflects the revolutionary nature of the Gospel. Dan has ventured where many would fear to tread."

♦ Jordan Wolley, President of *E412 Global* – *recruiting, equipping, and sending missionaries*

"Dan has wielded the tools of biblical scholarship to construct this ... captivating account – a 'shirt sleeve,' simple story of a small man who is given a big role in eternity.

"This is a terrific read and is ultimately as convicting as anything I have ever read."

♦ David Ware, Pastor and creator of *The Template: A Blueprint for Full Spectrum Ministry*

"If you have ever wondered about the judgment of believers at the Judgment Seat of Christ, this is a must read. In *The Reckoning*, Dr. Dan Lee draws the reader into the room through the eyes of a Christian [who is actually there]. This story will beg you to examine your daily actions as you experience the depth of God's grace in heartache and regret, and the celebration of an obedient and fruitful life. Bottom Line ... What you do today matters. Well done, Dan."

♦ Blake Lawhon, author of *When Grey Gets in the Way*

Praise for author's biblical scholarship

"Dan has played a key role in adult teaching and shepherding. He is a critical thinker ... and unique scholarly talent. Powerful ability to communicate God's truth."

♦ Dr. Andy McQuitty, Senior Pastor & author of *The Way to Brave: Shaping a David Faith in a Goliath World*

"Dan['s] knowledge and gentle guiding with the scriptures is unsurpassed. Life-altering for our congregation."

♦ Dr. Suzanne Castle, Senior Pastor & author of *Brim: Creative Overflow in Worship Design*

The Reckoning
at
Christ's Throne ~
One Pilgrim's Progress
to Triumph

Dan Lee, PhD

V1b

The Reckoning:
At Christ's Throne ~ One Pilgrim's Progress to Triumph

www.wordforge.drdanlee.com
Mineral Wells, Texas

Contact author at:
dan@drdanlee.com

ISBN: 978-0-9996917-9-3
Library of Congress Control Number: 2019916064

V1b

Acknowledgements:

My heartfelt thanks to my wife and ministry partner, Betsi, and to my friend and churchlife colleague, Dave, for their many hours spent reading this manuscript with careful eyes ... and for their many challenges to consider new story elements or better illuminate existing ones.

CONTENTS

Prologue

Scripture tells us a judgment for Christians is coming (2 Cor 5:9-10, Luke 19:12-27, 1 Cor 3:13-15, 1 Cor 9:24-27). This proceeding is not the Great White Throne Judgment, where unbelievers are eternally separated from God (Rev 20:11-15). Rather, it's a proceeding known to theologians as the Judgment Seat of Christ (2 Cor 5:9-10, Rom 14:10 NKJV). It will be conducted by Jesus upon His return to the Earth (Luke 19:12-27, Rev 22:12).

Despite the clear proclamation of this judgment in the New Testament, the modern church seems to have little awareness of it. Some well-intentioned Christians may question the reality of such a tribunal: "But aren't we saved by grace?" – the query goes. Indeed we are, but we are still accountable as servants (1 Cor 4:2, 3:11-15; Luke 19:12-27, 12:48b). The Judgment Seat of Christ is not about *where* we will spend eternity, but about *what we will do* in eternity, what part we will play.

Eternity is far vaster, far more engaging, far more alive with dynamic activity, than most of us have imagined.[1] In eternity, we'll be given the opportunity to shine forth for Christ ... and we will shine for Him precisely to the extent that we have shone for Him in our present lives (Dan 12:3; 2 Cor 9:6, 4:17; Luke 19:12-27, 16:9-11; 2 Tim 2:12 TPT; Rev 2:26-27).

This short story is a fictional account of what it may be like to appear before the Judgment Seat of Christ. The tale, while imaginary, is carefully grounded in the truth of scripture. The story seeks to capture both the thrill and the gravity of Christ's judgment of His own children.

The book also seeks to give you a tangible sense of the excitement and grandeur of the glorious eternity that will follow Christ's tribunal. Finally, the story hopes to awaken your imagination with a burning awareness of the impact that your life now will have on your role then.

If, as you're reading, you reach a moment in which you wonder, "Is that right?" or say to yourself, "I haven't heard that before," please refer to the associated endnotes for a biblical explanation. These notes are intended to authenticate the details of the narrative by pointing to the passages in scripture which support the concepts and images depicted.

Chapter 1: Awe

As Benny entered the Great Hall for the first time, he was startled by its simplicity. Instead of columns adorned with precious metals and carved with intricate designs, there were smooth, lightly curved columns of plain white stone. Instead of a ceiling of painted panels and carved reliefs, the overhead scene was mostly open – open to a gently shimmering sky of rich blues, with intermittent silvery whites. It was a fitting heavenward view for a new world. This was the restored Earth, where skies were perpetually calm and clear.[2]

Inside the hall, the entire space was subtly alive with the sound of soft voices from all quarters. The soothing chatter, while gently spirited, was also very hushed. It was as if the mellow timbre of the many voices was deliberately marking both the solemnity and the excitement of the proceeding that was about to take place.

The hall was composed primarily of pure, brilliant marble. It was the material of the floor, of the support pillars, and even of the ceiling beams that held the expansive glassy panels above. As a result, the hall carried a faint, pleasant smell of freshly buffed stone. Intermingled with the earthy aroma of the marble was the scent of white lilies and purple asters. These flowers adorned the hall's wide entrance – the lilies symbolizing Christ's resurrection power and the asters His royal dominion.

Benny looked slowly toward the far end of the immense room, taking in its vast dimensions as his eyes moved the full distance. He could just make out Jesus, the King of Kings, seated at the extreme end. Benny was so far away from Jesus that Jesus's body was little more than a stick figure to Benny's eyes. Despite the distance, Benny could see that Jesus was sitting on a rather unpretentious throne of white woods and silver trim. Warm light was radiating from Jesus's body and permeated the entire chamber; it was simultaneously brilliant and serene.[3]

Benny shouldn't have been overly surprised by the simple appearance of this throne hall. It wasn't built to bring attention to itself, but to its Owner. And, although Benny was unaware of it, he was himself a sort of microcosm of the hall. He was a simple man who hadn't sought to bring attention to himself, but to his Owner.

Benny wasn't concerned with titles or prestige; nor had he ever possessed any status that would draw others to him. He had worked as a manual laborer, a modest fabricator and welder, most of his career. He was a quiet man who, even in church settings, had worked primarily with his hands. He'd never been especially articulate and wasn't prone to speak often. Yet he was known for speaking the truth with wisdom and compassion when he did speak. Benny himself was only vaguely aware of his reputation for living out the love of Jesus with both his service and his words.

This is not to say Benny was without flaws; he was all too aware of his own failings – sometimes overly sensitive, sometimes protective of his ego, sometimes testy when things weren't going his way. But Benny had also always been quick to apologize and to work to restore relationships.

Benny had died peacefully at 88, essentially of old age. His medical file officially reported his cause of death as congestive heart failure, but his body, like his spirit, was just ready for the next chapter. Benny had died a contented man, surrounded by family and church friends and eager to see Jesus. And today, *this* day, he was standing in the very presence of the resurrected Jesus.

Benny too was now in a resurrected body.

Benny tore his thoughts and attention from the central figure in the room long enough to look around the Great Hall with a wider focus. There were people meandering throughout – some talking, and others making their way to the stadium-style seats that surrounded the main floor.

During this brief survey of the massive room, Benny noticed more shining bodies in addition to Jesus (though none as dazzling). Four figures, who stood not far from the entrance, had bodies with a warm yellowish glow. They each had facial features very distinct from one another, yet their forms shared a common attribute: they were all translucent, as if their physical frames were composed largely of light. They stood perhaps eight feet tall on average, and Benny recognized them as angels.[4] He had seen angels before, though not of this particular rank.

It was obvious to Benny, however, that more than Jesus and the angels were radiating splendorous light. He moved toward the center of the room to get a better look.

Chapter 2: Warmth

As Benny walked to the midpoint of the massive chamber, he realized the individuals seated in the floor area nearest Christ's throne radiated the brightest (apart from Jesus himself).[5] They sat on large, well-appointed chairs that bore what appeared to be individual names on their high backs. The glow from each figure was unique. Some shone in almost pure white, others in warm reds and purples, still others in hues of lively blues or greens.[6]

Benny was now at the center of the hall and could see that these figures were ordinary men and women ... all with kind, wise faces. Yet they varied significantly in ethnicity, height, and build.

Benny next took in the whole audience for a second time. They were slowly filling in the stadium seating above the floor area. He noticed most were not glowing – although here and there he could see a luminescent body. These softly shining folk were generally talking excitedly to someone, as if catching up with an old friend.

Everyone, luminescent or not, appeared to be in their late thirties or early forties. However, Benny knew this was not an indication of how long they'd lived, but was rather an artifact of their new resurrection bodies. Their forms, like his, had been reforged to perfection.

One of the yellow-glow angels quietly informed Benny he needed to take a seat in the general gallery until his name was called. The angel suggested he sit in the west-central section of the hall. This inviting figure told him he would probably find several of his friends there.

The angel's voice took Benny back (very briefly in his memory) to the last few hundred years and to his first encounter with angels. Benny had passed into Heaven about 240 years before this special day.[7]

At the time of his passing, it felt to Benny as if he had simply fallen asleep for a peaceful afternoon nap.[8] He'd then gently awakened to the warm evening lights of paradise.[9] Since that time, Benny had been living in God's expansive estate, Heaven. And he had resided there, in spirit form,[10] until about three months ago.

While in Heaven, Benny had met many angels and had gotten to know something about their lives ... not just their lives in God's celestial city, but their earlier lives among the stars (or "in the heavens," as they typically described it).[11] They had resided in the galaxies before arriving in Heaven.[12] Benny had grown fond of several of them and looked forward to spending more time with them in the future.

Benny was now no longer in Heaven, however. And he no longer existed in the spirit form in which he'd lived during his time there. He was, instead, in a delightful, new physical body.[13]

When Jesus had returned to the Earth, He'd brought Benny, along with everyone else who had fallen asleep as a child of God, back with Him. During this joyful, homecoming plunge to Earth, they had all taken on resurrection bodies. The episode felt like a graceful leap into a refreshing pool of water after so long a time without a physical form.[14]

During their descent many others joined them. These were God's children pulled up, living, from Earth. Just as Benny had been transformed during his descent, the newcomers had been transformed during their rise to meet Jesus.[15] They had all closed ranks in the skies.[16] And all now had tangible, physical, resurrected bodies. Benny felt very complete – very snug and at home – in this new body.[17] He knew it was where he belonged for the long, pleasant journey of eternity on which he was now about to embark.

When the family of God had initially returned, only Jesus had a body that radiated light. But during the months since their homecoming, Benny had occasionally glimpsed, from a distance, what he thought were other humans with shining bodies. Benny had been living in the suburbs of Jerusalem (the city in which this grand chamber stood) and had periodically made his way into the heart of the great town. It was there he had caught sight of gleaming, apparently human figures. He was delighted now, as he made his way to the section the usher angel had pointed him toward, to see it was unmistakably true.

Jerusalem, the capital of the new Earth, was simply called "Ariel" by most of its citizens now.[18] This restored city was a place of fantastic beauty, with gardens and streams, with fragrant aromas from flowers and trees, and with the soft hum of people engaged in all kinds of handmade crafts. But at this point the restored Jerusalem was only a shadow of the ultimate New Jerusalem that was to come.[19]

The current revitalized Jerusalem was being reconstructed primarily by angels.[20] They were much faster than humans and were nearly finished building. Their capacity was especially remarkable since *this* Jerusalem was many times larger than the old Jerusalem.[21] In fact, it extended well out into what was once the Mediterranean Sea ... which was now mostly dry land.[22]

The waters of the Mediterranean, like the waters of the all of Earth's oceans, had been partially dried up by the hand of God after the cataclysmic events of the Apocalypse.[23] The Holy Spirit, under the direction of Jesus, had drawn up much of the waters of the seas to recreate the vapor canopy that once covered the Earth.[24] As in the days before Noah and the great flood, the protective canopy now stood, unbroken and secure, high in the stratosphere.[25]

As a result of the canopy's presence, a new earthly order was beginning to take shape. The canopy had brought perpetually serene weather, as well as plentiful and regular moisture for agriculture and drinking water.

And there were rumors that natural life was also changing because of the canopy. Anecdotal reports claimed vegetation across the globe was morphing to contain all the flavors and nutrients many carnivores needed.[26] As a result, some predators were apparently becoming plant eaters and ceasing to be predatory.[27]

Aesthetically, the canopy also caused the sun's light to shimmer subtly and to diffuse just a little (without diminishing its intensity). The vapor of the canopy created rich and diverse blue tones throughout the entire sky. Clouds were now rare, and when they did appear, they were a wispy silver. All these changes gave the heavens a regal, yet soft and inviting, feel.

The new sky, viewed through the open ceiling of the Great Hall (as Benny was now observing it), was a delightful and wonderful sight. The Hall was, itself, one of the first works of the angelic builders. And Benny knew why. This chamber was Christ's throne room for his rule of the Earth, and it was currently being used day after day for the grand event known to everyone as the Judgment Seat of Christ.[28] Today was Benny's day, along with those of his period and place, to give an account of their lives to Jesus.

The Reckoning

Chapter 3: Rapport

As Benny approached the portion of the Great Hall the angel had directed him toward, he began to identify many familiar faces. Some were good friends; others acquaintances from his city; still others people he recognized because they were well-known in his regional area.

Timothy Crushmann

He identified Tim Crushmann in the first row of the section. Tim was a pastor Benny had once met ... when Benny had attended a worship event at Tim's church. The church seated several thousand, and it had been overflowing the night Benny was there. As Benny recalled, that particular night had also been one to remember. There was a full orchestra present, and the music was powerful and soul-refreshing.

Meanna Star

Seated beside Tim, Benny saw Mea Star, a very dynamic woman who had worked closely with Tim and other pastors of very large churches. Mea had been the founder and leader of a Christian organization called The Heart's Home. The expression on Mea's face let Benny know she was looking forward to today's events with keen expectation. Her ministry had been a huge success, and Benny felt Mea had good reason to be filled with anticipation. He knew that today King Jesus was going honor – with roles of enduring impact – those who has been faithful to him with their lives.[29]

Carson Monger

In the very next row, Benny noticed his friend Carson. The two had shared an interest in three-wheeled vehicles, and Benny had crossed paths with Carson often at displays and events. But they had never been very close. Benny was sure Carson had thought him rather boring while they were still in mortal bodies. Carson was a gregarious, party guy and seemed to live a pretty highrolling life. Benny wasn't even sure Carson was a Christian, but guessed he must be, if he was sitting in the hall for this event. He wondered why Carson had chosen to sit so close to the front, but chalked it up to Carson's flamboyance. Benny caught Carson's eye, waved somewhat diffidently, smiled hesitantly, and then continued toward the back of the section.

Joshua Selfmore

As Benny continued to climb the stairs, he saw an old college friend in the fourth row. Josh and Benny had been in the same dorm as freshmen, and they'd sometimes played ping-pong or foosball in the dorm commons. They would occasionally make a run to the local coffee shop together. Neither had had much money for anything else.

During their conversations, Josh had gotten Benny interested in examining the claims of Jesus. And as a result of these chats, Benny had eventually come to believe in Christ as his Redeemer. Benny and Josh had lost touch when Benny dropped out of college after his sophomore year to go to trade school.

As Benny approached the row where Josh was seated, he stopped to shake Josh's hand and then kept climbing the stairs.

Kenneth Songlow

Across the aisle from Josh, and a couple rows farther back, Benny spotted Ken Songlow. Ken had been a very successful American businessman. Benny didn't know him personally, but knew Ken had a heart for the disadvantaged. Ken had been well-known in charity circles, because he'd devoted much of his energy and resources to reconciliation and uplift ministries on the Korean peninsula after the reunification of North and South.

Benny saw several other people he knew as he continued up the stairs. A few were colleagues from his work. One was a neighbor from his last suburban street. Others were members of his church. He stopped to exchange hugs with a few of them.

Jane Savage

Among these friends, he noticed Jane Savage. Jane had attended Benny's church for a long time, but had eventually moved to a more conventional congregation. She had always seemed a bit churchy to Benny, but he'd felt at the time it was simply because she was older and preferred time-honored hymns and worship traditions. Benny had admired her heavy involvement in discipling others and her incredible command of the Bible. It seemed as if she had memorized almost the entire thing.

Benny greeted Jane and then made his way to an upper row that was still only about a quarter full. He decided to enter it.

Gale Willow

To his surprise, Benny saw his ex-wife, Gale, sitting in the row, toward the far aisle. He had run into her in Heaven several times over the years. They had even had a couple of indepth conversations reflecting on their years together and on the years after their divorce. During these exchanges, they had both reacknowledged their failures in the marriage. They had also put away any lingering resentful feelings.

Benny smiled at Gale, but was uncertain whether it would be wise to sit with her for this hearing. He felt they might both get a "come-to-Jesus" scolding for the divorce on this day of accountability. Perhaps it would be better, Benny thought, to avoid the temptation to compare notes afterward.

Benny and Gale had been unable to have children. And Benny had remained single after their 28 years together. But Gale had remarried a few years following the breakup – with a long and, by her own account, happy marriage. Benny had met Gale's second husband, Jim, only once, and that was in Heaven. Benny didn't know whether the two had been particularly close after "falling asleep," but surmised Jim had simply not yet entered the hall.

William and Bethany Servunto

As Benny made his way deeper into the row, he also saw Will and Beth Servunto sitting about midway. Will and Beth were a couple he had gotten to know well during their earthly lives together; they were about twenty years his senior. Benny decided to sit next to them. They stood and hugged him warmly.

Will and Beth were still best friends, despite the fact that marriage did not continue into eternity.[30] Benny had seen the two together regularly in Heaven. They had been missionaries to Borneo, and Benny's church had supported them. Benny had always invited them to stay in his home whenever they were in town.

As Benny took a seat beside them, he recalled that they had produced very few converts and even fewer disciples in Borneo. He silently wondered what kind of honor they would receive from King Jesus and the assembled company with so little to show for their effort.

Then Benny's thoughts turned to his own life. He found himself happy just to be in this great gathering of believers. He had sought to live for His Lord, but knew he'd not had the kind of influence Mea Star, Pastor Tim, or even the Servuntos had had. How would he fare in front of the King of Kings? He was not particularly optimistic, especially given his gut-level consciousness of his sometimes-repetitive failures. However, he greatly looked forward to the chance to speak face to face with Jesus again, whatever the outcome.

Chapter 4: Gravitas

As the time came for the day's event to begin, Benny noticed the uppermost portions of the grand auditorium filling with angels. Shortly thereafter two archangels, one on either side of Christ's throne, blew into massive, harmonizing horns.[31] *Archangels*, as distinct from more typical angels, were recognizable by their size and hue (as Benny had learned in Heaven). These two had changed their appearance for this trumpeting event; they looked perfectly solid and had enormous wings.[32]

Benny knew from his time in Heaven that when angels manifested wings it was not to take flight, but to amplify focus. Angels didn't need wings to fly. Rather, when they shapeshifted[33] and presented wings, it was to arrest visual attention. Wings were like outstretched hands on a grand scale – they were a big gesture that said, "Behold this."

Each of the two archangels spread one wing just behind the throne … and they did so in such a way that their wings overlapped at the tips. The other wing they spread out over the closest of those brightly shining humans seated around Jesus.

The entire company of angels in the immense room then burst into song. They sang in the Ayewellic tongue. It was the chief language of the angels and the common language of Heaven.[34] Because all the humans in the hall had been in Heaven for at least two centuries, they had all learned Ayewellic long ago and quickly joined in the song of worship to the King of Kings.

When the singing was complete, Jesus stood up and addressed the entire assembly. Though His voice was gentle and soft, it resonated throughout the enormous space. Benny felt as if his Redeemer were standing right next to him.

"Welcome, precious ones," Jesus began. "I've had time to talk to every one of you already during our time together in Heaven. But this is a special day in which I'll have a more penetrating and deliberate exchange with each of you.

"We, together – by returning to establish this City of Light, Ariel[35] – have begun in earnest the enterprise of uniting Heaven and Earth.[36] I'm your Captain in this endeavor,[37] and you are my figurative bride. That means you are *the Eternal King's bride* ... which also means you are the queen who will gently rule with Me.[38] Our task over the next millennium will be to restore the Earth to the beauty, peace, justice and warmth My Father intend when he first created it.[39]

"Once our work is complete, our Father will join us here. Heaven will descend and become the New Jerusalem.[40] God the Father will live among us, and Heaven and Earth will truly, literally be one. Our Father has had this union in mind from the beginning."[41]

"Today, as you are all now aware, you'll receive your assignments[42] – not only for the great restoration I just described, but for the task of sustaining the Kingdom of Light[43] once the Father has come to live with us here."

"While you can legitimately look on your appointment today as a return on your investment of living faithfully for Me,[44] your upcoming role in the Kingdom is, above all, about being empowered to live in the fullness of your identity as a child of God. I'm the Shepherd King, and I created each one of you to be a companion shepherd leader – caring for My creation with me."[45]

"If you've grown spiritually to become the mature son or daughter I intended you to be, you will be unleashed to shine forth with My character, influence, and love.[46] But these qualities must already be flourishing within you. You must have already developed the *heart* of a shepherd[47] ... *if* you are to be anointed this day to be the *shepherd of creation* I conceived you to be."[48]

"You should be aware that Satan's rebellion placed the angelic realm in as much disarray as the human realm.[49] As a result, some of you will be assigned as governors of angelic civilizations.[50] Rest easy. I know each of you well, and you'll only be given such a role if I've sensed a deep passion for that kind of adventure in your soul."

"For the sake of clarity, recognize that this hearing is the event known in the New Testament as 'The Judgment Seat of Christ.' It's distinct from the Great White Throne Judgment, which you've also read about in scripture. That tribunal will not occur for another thousand years or so.[51] At that judgment, you will not even be present. When your name is called at the Great White Throne, the throne of My Father, I will stand in your place. That's because, in the eyes of His justice, you are completely covered and shielded by Me."

"Today, you will each be called down to the front, together with a group of your contemporaries. The rest of this assembly will hear and see everything that's happening, but those in your smaller circle will be able to ask questions or make comments during your life's examination."

"You may be wondering who these few hundred shining people here in front with Me are," Jesus said. He then made a doublehanded sweeping gesture toward the luminous ones around his chair. "They are the senior shepherd leaders for My Kingdom. They are the kings, queens, and governors of the *Kingdom of Light* – the kingdom we are here to establish and sustain."

"They now radiate brilliant light from their bodies – because they shone brightly for me when they served me in the first creation.[52] A few of you will be joining them today and will shine as vividly as they do."

"Each of you, once your resurrected body has been augmented today, will shine in accordance with the measure of My spiritual light you displayed in your original body of mortal flesh."[53]

Jesus swept his hand again over the shining ones in front of Him, and continued: "These elder shepherds, these pillars of our new Jerusalem community, are my inner council and have helped me decide the assignments you'll receive today.[54] I must warn you that some of you have not prepared yourselves for any kind of responsibility here, and others have displayed profound disregard for the way I wanted you to be and to live in the world. If you're one of these, you'll be assigned to live and work in a distressed, still-desperate place[55] ... even as we work gradually and deliberately to restore that place and every corner of the Earth. This will be your opportunity to develop the qualities I intended you to manifest to the world around you the first time."[56]

"Before we begin, you may have some general questions. You'll notice that, while I've been talking, angels have made their way into the aisles and are stationed at the ends of each row. They're there to answer questions you may have about this proceeding. However, they won't be able to answer inquiries about your specific evaluation or possible assignment."

Jesus then ended with one final practical note: "You may be concerned about the time it will take to appraise everyone here. And you may wonder how that could delay us in getting on with our task of rebuilding creation to meet our

Father's original desire. Know this: time is compressed in this chamber, and we'll complete everyone's review in the space of a single day."

Benny turned and saw an angel standing at the end of the row. Hesitatingly, he softly motioned the angel toward him. The figure smiled, and Benny knew immediately it was okay that he had signaled.

As the angel approached, Benny recognized her. It was Stareweanni; he had met her about 125 years earlier during an exceptional worship gathering in Heaven. Seeing her brought back memories of the first time he had encountered a female angel. It was on the streets of Heaven in his early weeks there. And it had surprised him. He had been led to believe angels were genderless.[57]

Many weeks later, at his first opportunity, he had asked Elagollin, an angel who was male in appearance and who had befriended him early on, about this. Elagollin let out a hearty laugh and then explained: "Many people arrive here with that misconception. But just like humans, we angels were originally fashioned to procreate.[58] Also just like humans, when we were privileged to enter Heaven, the sexual part of our nature changed. We still possess gender, but not sexuality."[59]

Stareweanni had now arrived by Benny's side and looked at him inquisitively.

"I have just a couple of quick questions," Benny said. "First, if everyone waiting to be judged today has yet to be glorified with shining radiance, why are some people in the audience already glowing?"

"Simple," Stareweanni said, "they've already been appraised ... and for most of them, that was yesterday. Yesterday was the day those living in the generation before today's group were evaluated. The people you see shining are here to support someone they had a special relationship with – perhaps a young person they mentored or a grandchild who followed in their faith."

Benny was pleased by this, realizing it must mean Jesus thought it was important for the generations of His people to be connected. It was, after all, Benny remembered, one church, one faith, one bride.

Benny moved on to his second question: "Did Jesus mean it literally when he said we wouldn't stand at the Great White Throne Judgment? Or was that just figurative language to tell us we don't need to be worried about it?"

"No, he meant it," she replied. "At that judgment you are completely hidden within Jesus – in courtroom terms, that is. So, even if you were to attend in person, God the Father wouldn't consider your presence. Judicially, He will only recognize Jesus standing in your place. There is absolutely no need for you to be there personally. Consequently, today's judgment is the only one you ever will undergo."

Someone else called Stareweanni over, and Benny was left with his thoughts for a few minutes.

Then the archangels beside Christ's throne blew their trumpets again and everyone's eyes turned once more to the front of the hall.

Chapter 5: Anticipation

One of the trumpeting archangels, with wings now folded, read out a list of about twenty names. Occasionally the angel would include a birthdate with a name. Benny guessed this was because more than one person with that same name was currently in the Great Hall. Benny watched as those who had been called made their way to the front. He noticed that, for the most part, they had already been together, sitting in a wide clump. It seemed each person was being called down with those who knew them best in life.

Once the small group was assembled in front of the throne, Jesus called the first name, a Candice Stables, to come forward. Candice flinched with a start, then somewhat nervously stepped up and onto the low platform so that she was just in front of Jesus. Benny didn't know Candice, but his eyes were absolutely glued to her. Like everyone in the hall, he was trying to get a better feel for the proceeding from this first sample. Candice was their guinea pig. She appeared apprehensive, and the entire assembly shared her uneasy excitement.

"Welcome, Candice," Jesus began, with a kind smile. "You're here because you're My redeemed child. You needn't have any fear about your longterm future in the Kingdom of Light – *regardless* of what happens during this evaluation.[60] You'll spend the whole of eternity living in the joy of My renewed creation. And you'll have the opportunity to visit and speak with Me at regular intervals."[61]

The two archangels then flew gracefully upward to mount large, twelve-foot pedestals adjacent to Jesus's throne. Once atop the pedestals, the angels were just aft of, and a somewhat higher than, Christ's great chair. They each spread their wings, one wing upward and one downward. Between their outstretched wings, as if on a transparent screen, a moving image of Candice at about age 18 appeared. It was a 3D, holographic-style image, only much more solid.

On the screen, select parts of Candice's life played out. It was the story of the things Candice had done during her life to honor God, to show Christ's love to others, and to care for His creation. There were several clips of Candice caring for animals, especially horses.

Benny wondered why very little negative footage appeared; had Candice been an unusually sin-free woman?

Occasionally the archangels would stop the playback, and it became apparent this was happening because Candice or someone else in the group had a question. The final scene of the video was of Candice as she lay on her deathbed. She was, at that point, an old woman with kindness in her face, and she was describing to friends the sweet fellowship she was having with her Lord.

As the sequences came to a close, Jesus said, "Candice, overall you have been a faithful servant, though you should have been more deeply committed to serving people in addition to animals. But you did manifest a giving, unselfish heart. Your senior shepherd will be the Apostle Bartholomew, and he'll be assigning you a role shepherding a community of zebras."

"Someone else will serve as your immediate leader. That person will oversee your work as a guiding shepherd between you and Bartholomew. I want you to focus on building a caring relationship with him or her, not just a working relationship. That person has already been identified, but I won't announce their name yet, because they aren't going stand where you're standing until a few days from now. "

"Lord Jesus," Candice replied, "I realize from my time in Heaven that you wanted me to be as loving and attentive toward people as animals – even though people had such capacity to hurt me. But I'm very grateful for this fantastic role. I'm so excited to get started, to help restore Your creation."

Jesus smiled again at Candice and, with an open-handed gesture toward her, said, "Your body will now shine with the same kindness and truth you radiated in your first life." Immediately Candice's body took on a subtle, earthy green glow.

The entire hall breathed a collective sigh of relief. With this first review complete, everyone had little better idea of what to expect from the day.

Chapter 6: Dismay

Several groups were then called in which Benny knew no one. As he watched, he wondered at a pattern he was seeing emerge. Very rarely had anyone done much that was sinful during their lives. At least, if they had, it wasn't showing up on the big screen.

Then a group was summoned by the archangels that included Josh Selfmore, the man who had befriended Benny in college and who had led him to Christ. As Josh moved toward the front, Benny recalled that Josh had studied aeronautical engineering. Benny had known Josh to be an exceptional and very diligent university student.

Benny had run into Josh in Heaven after a few decades there. They had arranged to meet several times since then – at various garden spots around Heaven – and Benny had gotten much of Josh's story during those conversations.

After college Josh had joined a major aerospace firm. He'd had a very successful professional career, finishing his working years as the company's Director for Advanced Technologies Research. Benny had known Josh to be a fair, principled, and approachable guy and was sure he'd run a high-integrity department.

Josh was about the twelfth person in the group to be invited forward. Benny knew that Josh had remained consistent in church during most of his life, attending weekly for worship. Yet Josh's video was surprisingly short.

Some of the earliest footage was of his college conversations with Benny, which ultimately led to Benny's faith in Jesus. There were also other positive scenes of Josh's integrity in his professional life and of his patience and thoughtfulness toward his employees. He was also seen caring for his wife and two children.

In addition, there were clips of Josh achieving financial success. He wasn't excessively wealthy – at least, not by Western standards – but he was certainly able to build a pleasant, prosperous life.

Yet there were intermingled negative sequences. These surprised Benny ... given what he had seen as a pattern of the general, though not absolute, absence of such excerpts previously. Mixed among the images of professional success were episodes of Josh spending the overwhelming majority of his resources on creating a grand life for himself and his family.[62] Very little of his money, and almost none of his time, went to serving others or to advancing Christ's mission in the world.

There was a pause in the playback as Jesus commended Josh for a good work ethic. But Jesus also made clear that it was *He* who had blessed Josh. Benny used the short break to get Stareweanni's attention (the female angel who was still standing nearby). As she approached, Benny asked, "Why is there negative stuff in some people's life stories, but not in others?"

"Because," Stareweanni hurriedly replied, "this is a judgment about servanthood, not sinfulness.[63] In anyone's story, the harmful episodes are only recounted if they've created longstanding patterns of broken servanthood, such as poor stewardship with time, skill, or income."

Josh's story was now rolling again. The angelic screen showed him in worship services regularly, but conspicuously absent from most other activities in the life of his faith community. There was one nice scene near the end of Josh's 82 years that saw him again, for the second time in his life, telling another person about his faith in Christ – just as he had done with Benny.

Benny didn't know what to make of the video. But Jesus was about to clarify a few things for him.

"Josh," He said, "your life is typical of so many of your time who lived in the relative security and prosperity of Pax Americana. You generally conducted yourself morally and with integrity and even occasionally acted as My witness."

"But you were mostly focused on creating a magnificent, well-appointed life for yourself and your family.[64] I wanted your passion to be for My mission in the world and preparing for My Kingdom.[65] Instead your driving desire was to get the most out of your short life ... without, of course, resorting to dishonesty or unprincipled living. It was as if you imagined morality was all I expected of you."[66]

"Your heart was where your treasure was, firmly planted in earthly satisfaction.[67] You were primarily a consumer of Christianity, not a significant transmitter of my love. You sowed sparingly and so you will reap sparingly."[68]

Jesus went on: "But there is one thing you did well, Josh. You developed a temperament for treating people as valuable individuals and not merely as objects to accomplish your professional ends. You'll shepherd a small group of people, mostly younger people, who are struggling to find the discipline to be productive in society. In doing so you'll not only be helping them grow, but you'll learn the joy of truly pouring your heart into someone outside yourself and your natural loved ones. Your senior shepherd will be Queen Givingheart of Middle North America, once known as Sarah Nassar. There will be several levels of intermediate shepherd leaders between the two of you."

Josh interjected with a question: "Will these individuals I'm to shepherd be in resurrected bodies?"

"No," Jesus replied, "they are part of the world we've come to restore and are living in the city of New Orleans. They don't yet know Me as their Redeemer.[69] You'll live among them as their guide. Their city, like so many of Earth's old population centers, is recovering from the effects of the Father's judgment on the world that preceded our return to Earth.[70] You knew that judgment (now past) as the Apocalypse."

"Josh, the people you'll shepherd have great potential to rebuild their city and to recreate their society to meet our Father's vision. Incidentally, the climate there has already been restored to that of Earth's beginnings ... and is much different than when you visited the city as a tourist."

With a motion of his hand, Jesus caused Josh's body to shine at the same level of radiance with which Josh had flickered for Him, though only occasionally, in life. It was a rather dim glow and Josh moved toward the upper back portion of the auditorium. It seemed he knew instinctively at this point where he should be seated. As Josh walked past Benny in the nearest aisle, it was evident he was very reflective and deeply disappointed.[71]

Benny felt a twinge of sorrow for Josh, but was happy he had been given at least some shepherding responsibility in Christ's Kingdom.

The Reckoning

Chapter 7: Disappointment

The very next group called up after Josh's included megaministry leader, Mea Star. Mea was called forward fairly early from the bunch. She seemed eager and expectant. She'd led a tremendously successful ministry.

Benny knew quite a bit about Mea's parachurch organization, The Heart's Home. The ministry had helped many marriages grow and many women become more confident leaders and contributors in their homes, churches, and businesses. Benny had even attended a marriage conference that The Heart's Home had conducted at the Metropolitan Convention Center in his city. There must have been over 8,000 people in attendance, and the place had been abuzz with warmhearted energy. Benny felt it was a truly worthwhile experience.

Mea's story played out on the angelic screen with images of her as a cheerful, positive leader, who'd encouraged others and thought often about how to add value to their lives. There were scenes of the many successes of her ministry as it impacted lives.

The video revealed that Mea was also a compassionate leader within her organization. She was thoughtful, considerate, and slow to dismiss staff – giving them lots of opportunity for change and improvement.

She was a great speaker as well, showing vulnerability, humor, and much relational wisdom.

But there were also scenes of a different flavor. Some episodes showed Mea very distressed, even depressed, on occasions – when her message didn't resonate well with an audience or when she received what appeared to be well-intentioned criticism from a pastor or a pillar in the community.

Mea was seen basking in praise from her audiences and from celebrities (which included both secular personalities and churchworld luminaries). She would spend long hours gazing at awards she had gotten from organizations that admired vast international ministries. She seemed to live for the limelight.

From the footage, it also appeared that she was constantly finding ways to make her message more audience-pleasing, sometimes even avoiding biblical truths she knew might offend.

Mea's life replay saw her slowing down in her later years, handing over day-to-day operation of the ministry to younger women. But she was still very much loving the spotlight, as part of the speaking circuit. Her video closed with a sweet clip of her acknowledging the importance of Christ in her life as she "fell asleep in Him."

Benny wasn't sure what to think of her story. She had done so much good, yet those unflattering scenes must have been part of the narrative for a reason. Was her people-pleasing approach and desire for the approval of humans a significant hindrance to eternal servanthood, he wondered? He was about to find out.

"Mea," Jesus began, "your story is a mix of good results and poor motives. You must understand that shepherding in My eternal Kingdom is more about heart than visibility.[72] Even now you're hoping for a huge role, perhaps a mighty queenship, so everyone will adore you and see your greatness."

"I need shepherdesses who want to lead solely because they have a passion to be part of what I'm doing in the new creation. I must have guides who ache for a world filled with goodness, justice, and joyful devotion to My Father – guides who aren't consumed with the privileges and prominence of leadership. Can you honestly tell me that that describes you at this moment?"

Mea winced and shook her head meekly.

Jesus continued, now addressing the whole hall: "I cautioned you all, when I was here the first time, that if you were serving primarily for the sake of the admiration of humankind, you should not expect further reward. I let you know then that such admiration would *be* your reward. In short, motive matters a great deal."[73]

Then He turned again to Mea. "Nevertheless, Mea, I know you did love Me, even if often far less than yourself. And I perceive you can now serve with sincere intentions – provided that no grand, highly-visible title accompanies you. You'll be working for Governor Troy Montenegro as his Undersecretary for the Uplift of Women. You'll be stationed in the Sonora province of Old Mexico with him. You'll both be working under King Goodheart, originally called Sachi Serpentfeather, a Mayan by natural birth."

Mea thanked Jesus, though she couldn't hide her disappointment. But Benny sensed she was a woman who would quickly process what Jesus had said to her and get on with her new assignment with enthusiasm.

Mea began to glow pleasantly. And, although the evaluation wasn't what she had hoped for, the whole assembly of humans and angels clapped sweetly for her as she returned to the section where she had been seated. Mea didn't return to the front row, however; she took a seat a few rows back.

The day was turning out to hold more twists and unexpected turns than Benny could have imagined.

Chapter 8: Celebration

Two more groups, ones in which Benny did not know anyone, came and went. Then a small circle of folks was called forward which included Benny's missionary friends, Will and Bethany Servunto; they were sitting right next to him. Their little bunch also included a woman Benny recognized as Beth's sister.

After several people in this group stood before the throne, it was Bethany's turn. As she moved forward, Benny recalled the many pleasant encounters he'd had with her and her earthtime husband, Will, in Heaven. Benny had been stunned, once he had learned their final story, at how committed they'd been. Despite spending nearly thirty years in Borneo, they had seen less than a dozen people embrace Christ as Savior. And of those, only three or four had committed themselves to a faithful life of growth and service. Yet Beth, in particular, had been just as passionate about their mission the day she arrived in Heaven as the day she first landed in Borneo.

Jesus began speaking and started in the same way he had each time. "Welcome, Bethany. You're here because you are my redeemed child...."

Then the visual review of Beth's life began. It included, among other things, scenes of Beth in study, reflection and prayer. Much of this footage centered on her exploration of the lives of commendable women in scripture ... and on her heart work to conform her character to their likeness (which is also to say: to the essence of Jesus). In many ways, the remainder of her story was simply the outpouring of this vital interior growth.

There were a number of clips of Beth serving the villagers of Borneo in a variety of ways – from teaching them to read and sew to nursing wounds and animal bites. She was also seen leading a tiny handful to faith in Jesus over the years.

But the footage included more than just Beth and her work. There were snippets from the lives of those few converts who actually became committed disciples. These believers were shown – many years after Beth's time among them – expressing Christ's love and leading others to servanthood. Benny quickly realized these acts were included in Beth's story because they were the downstream effects of her spiritual investment in people. But even with these scenes, Beth's total results – in terms of numbers, at least – were still very small.

Beth interrupted at one point and said, "King Jesus, I'm sorry that I drew so few people to become your faithful disciples."

Jesus simply replied, "You planted and watered. It didn't matter to Me whether a tiny blueberry sprouted or a giant watermelon."[74]

As Beth's life excerpts continued, Benny, along with the whole assembly, also saw her faithfulness in her senior years – the years after she was too old to continue in the primitive environment of Borneo's villages. Yet she was still joyful and involved. She busied herself praying for, and encouraging, missionaries and pastors as they dealt with the challenges of demanding ministries.

At the end of the images, Jesus said, "Bethany, you've been a truly faithful servant, giving your whole life to Me – extremely well done.[75] Your work to develop the character of a godly woman not only impacted your life in time, but will be of tremendous value to me for all eternity. You'll join this group here beside My throne, these senior shepherds who intimately surround me. You'll be known from here onward as Queen Ferventheart."

"We're aware of your African-Somalian heritage, but also of your love for the people of Borneo. We've decided to give you a choice to shepherd Somalia or the island of Borneo. But you don't need to choose right now."

After a brief pause, Jesus continued: "Now, Queen Ferventheart, you will shine with the same radiance you manifested for me in your original, mortal body." Beth immediately began to radiate with dazzling brilliance ... like those already seated around the throne.

Jesus then turned to the audience and said, "Stand and welcome Queen Ferventheart. She'll be further honored at our great banquet tonight." Everyone stood, including Jesus himself,[76] and applauded Queen Ferventheart. The ovation was accompanied by whistles ... and by shouts of, "You go, girl!"

Next was Will Servunto's turn. His video was similar to Beth's, except it was painfully obvious that, as a seasoned elder, he was not the encourager to Christian leaders Beth had been.

Benny's mind went back briefly to the conversations he'd had in Heaven with Will and Beth. Benny had learned that Will had become somewhat sulky in their late years – when he realized their life's work had amounted to nothing more than a few believers and a couple of disciples. Will felt God should have rewarded them with bigger impact. He was even occasionally jealous of evangelists and missionaries who could count their impact in thousands or tens of thousands.

During one of these heavenly exchanges, Benny heard a soul-baring admission from Will: Will had come to realize, after many years in Heaven, that his negative attitude had robbed him of a measure of joy, of servanthood, and of full intimacy with Christ toward the end of his life.

As Will's later years were playing out on the overhead, Will asked to pause the footage for a moment – which drew

Benny's full attention back to the proceeding. Will meekly said, "Lord, I'm so sorry I let my own sense of self-importance reduce my capacity as a servant." Jesus simply looked at Will, then closed his eyes softly and pressed his lips lightly together in gentle remorse for Will.

Nevertheless, when the review was complete, Jesus looked at Will and said, "Will, despite some murky emotions toward the end, you've been a fairly faithful servant.[77] As you now know, you could have borne even more fruit, albeit quiet, unsung fruit, if you had simply embraced all I was asking of you. I wanted you to be completely devoted and joyful in making the smallest impact, so you could be faithful in very large impact now."[78]

"Still, the course of your life has been one of loyal servanthood, committed to Me and to others. You'll serve as a regional governor under your earthtime wife, who is now Queen Ferventheart (whether she chooses to shepherd in Borneo or Somalia)."

Will's face beamed. "My King," he said, "this is more opportunity for impact in Your Kingdom than I feel I deserve. And I'm delighted to be serving alongside the person who has been the closest to my soul both on Earth and in Heaven."

Will began to luminesce and was invited to take a seat on the first row of the section he had already been sitting in. An angel accompanied Will there and asked Tim Crushmann, the megachurch leader who'd been sitting in the front row, to move back a row to make way for Will.[79]

Benny wondered at this request to Tim, but he was coming to realize that many of the day's proceedings were not going to turn out as he'd anticipated.

Most of all, Benny felt genuine joy at the way his friends, Beth and Will, had been honored by Jesus and this great gathering of believers and angels. What eternal impact they were going to have!

Chapter 9: Gall

Another few sets of people went by. Then the summoning angel called a group which included Jane Savage. Jane was the woman Benny had esteemed for her vast command of scripture. He had known her only in her later years.

When it was Jane's turn, she stepped up to the throne confidently. She received the same sincere greeting from Jesus Benny had heard many times already this morning.

Then Jane's chronicle began to unfold. Benny was surprised to learn that she shared something in common with his good friends Will and Beth. Jane too had been a missionary. She had served in the southern Philippines for about fifteen years.

It was evident in her video that other women were drawn to Jane – whether she was overseas or stateside. She seemed well-grounded and clear in her life purpose. And she always knew the right thing to do in virtually every life circumstance. From the clips, Benny could tell her worship in song was real and zestful. And her prayers, both public and private, appeared authentic and anchored in a strong consciousness of God's character.

Jane's story was filled with many episodes of her skillfully discipling others with her profound awareness of scripture. She had unmistakable, Proverbs-like wisdom which was born from years of biblical study.

But it seemed from the footage, to Benny at least, that her priorities were sometimes misplaced. For example, she wanted the villagers in the Philippines to adopt Western clothing. As far as she was concerned, their native dress left them much too naked.

Jane was deeply concerned with teaching the tribal residents morality. Such instruction was an almost exclusive focus for her. She did little to impart to new converts gratitude for, or rest in, God's care and grace. As Benny watched, he thought to himself, "Morality is certainly a good thing, but this seems like lots of rules without much Spirit."

In the excerpts, Jane was often impatient with students who weren't reforming their lives quickly enough to meet her expectations. And she was particularly intolerant of believers who had been Christians for a long time, but who were struggling to live to biblical standards. Among other practices, she refused to go to the wedding of anyone who had been divorced in the past – and also typically ended her relationship with them following the new union.

Her intolerance applied especially to other missionaries. When she discovered a fellow missionary had had an affair or other dishonorable episode in their past, she was ready to stop working with them altogether.

In one scene in her life's playback, a young female pastor asked her about this approach to the faith community. Jane said she felt God wanted her, and all of us, to carry His standard everywhere and to continue to sound the message of the Old Testament prophets concerning sin and disobedience. To Jane's credit, she herself was, as a rule, living to the guidelines she demanded of others.

As Jane's life story came to a close, she was portrayed on the big screen still discipling women who were attracted to her well-ordered, stable life. But, generally, only the most stalwart were able to stay with her in the long run.

Benny studied Jane's face as the video wrapped up. It was evident she was, for the most part, gratified. She exuded a sureness, a certainty that she'd been doing the Lord's work. Did Benny have it wrong, he wondered? Surely, Jane, with her depth of biblical wisdom, would, of all people, know what God desired from His servants.

Jesus now spoke. "Dear Jane," he groaned softly, "I know you love me, and you had a passion for My Word and My work. Your grasp of scripture is truly admirable. But can you not see that I needed you to have the same soft spot in your heart for My people as for My Word? Your judgmental approach was oppressive to many struggling Christians."

"You were right to want My people to live righteously. But *I* am the prophet I hoped you would imitate. I'm the Prophet who wept for Jerusalem,[80] the Prophet who said 'Come to me, you who are weary and burdened down ... for I'm gentle and humble in heart, and you'll find rest.'[81] You forgot tenderness, Jane."[82]

"But Lord," Jane protested, "I was defending Your honor and Your law." She was visibly vexed, displeased.

Jesus replied: "I called you to be salt and light,[83] not an anvil and hammer. You confused the verbal message the ancient prophets were to proclaim with the message your life and heart were supposed to declare."

"Furthermore, My prophets of old harbored no smugness in delivering those messages. They recognized that they themselves were unworthy, and they mourned deeply over the sins of their people."[84]

"I and my inner circle of senior shepherds have struggled to know how to use you. Biblical wisdom and prophetic exhortation, without kindheartedness, are of little value in building My Kingdom of Goodness.[85] You'll have only an indirect shepherding role.[86] You'll be an advisor to Governor Gentleheart, who'll be shepherding Washington, D. C. – a place filled with people you once disdained. But you now will find yourself investing deeply in their lives with your wisdom. That wisdom will be filtered, however, through Governer Gentleheart's spirit of patience and tenderness.

With a wave of Jesus's hand, Jane's body began to shine, but not nearly as brightly as it could have.

The Reckoning

Chapter 10: Shame

The very next group called up after Jane's included Carson Monger. Carson was Benny's casual friend who shared his interest in three-wheeled vehicles – but who seemed to distance himself from Benny's dullness.

Jesus welcomed Carson warmly – intensely, genuinely – just as he had everyone, and affirmed Carson's status as an everlasting child of God with a permanent place in His eternal Kingdom.

But Carson's life story was hard to watch. Carson looked at the floor almost the entire time. He had trusted in Jesus in his mid-twenties, and for a period of about a year he had been involved in a small community of disciples. But he'd quickly returned to life on his own terms. As the clips revealed, he was a lifelong womanizer and extreme partier. It was obvious he'd lived for fleshly pleasure.

Carson had owned a successful construction business, but it was also clear from the start that Carson was essentially a conman. He was very charming and used his charisma regularly to take advantage of others. He was clever enough to stay just above the law, making arrangements with handshakes and verbal assertions – avoiding written contracts wherever possible. He switched subcontractors constantly and routinely failed to pay them all they were owed. He cut corners and then lied to clients about what was actually going on behind the scenes. He drove staff to leave on an almost quarterly basis because he didn't fulfill his promises to them.

He was a master of temporary arrangements – which allowed him to continually start over with fresh, new, unsuspecting faces. Carson was even willing to falsely accuse others when he felt it necessary to accomplish his goals. He certainly lacked the business integrity of Benny's college friend, Josh.

Benny was surprised at how much ugliness and sinful behavior was evident in these images. At one point Carson even requested that the replay be paused and asked why he hadn't seen so much damaging material in other people's videos. Benny immediately recalled Stareweanni's words about sinful behavior and its effects on servanthood.

Jesus looked at Carson and drew his breath in a long, painful sigh. "Carson, other people *did* engage in some of the same vicious behaviors we've seen here. But among those whose lives we've reviewed so far, they all followed the behavior with something you lacked. They recognized the harm they'd caused and did what they could to heal the wounds they'd inflicted.[87] You were calloused, selfish, unrepentant. You made no attempt at restoration or restitution. Some people carried the hurts you inflicted for the rest of their lives. Others were turned off toward me for years, even decades, knowing you were a Christian."

"Because you were not a reconciler, the schemes you hatched in private and the slanderous comments you made behind closed doors are now being shouted from the rooftops, as it were."[88]

After this exchange between the two, the playback continued only briefly until reaching its end. By now, Carson's rather desperate show of indignation had turned to utter shame.[89] "Jesus, I'm terribly sorry that I made no attempt to be your representative or your follower in any way. I realize now I don't even deserve to be standing in this hall."

"Carson," came Jesus's reply, "no one in this room deserves to be here. They're here because, like you, they trusted in Me to redeem them. You'll spend eternity in my Kingdom of Light, but you've been completely useless to Me as a servant.[90] In fact, the enduring 'testimony' of your life as a whole caused Me substantial harm."

"Your spiritual birth reforged you,[91] and you became a complete human with a living spirit.[92] As such, you had the capacity to develop into a wonderfully bright reflection of My image. But you absolutely squandered that potential."[93]

"As a result of your total failure to prepare your character and your heart, you'll have no shepherding role at all.[94] Additionally, you must learn a true spirit of respect and kindness for others. You'll be sent for a very long season to live in a community in Uttar Pradesh, India, where many people are still oppressed.[95] They struggle under the same disregard you showed others – though they're experiencing that disregard at its extreme, in the form of modern human slavery."[96]

"Your life among them will be austere and arduous for some centuries to come.[97] Eventually Queen Justheart of India will successfully and fully renew this part of My Kingdom. She is My faithful servant, formerly called Tahira Gulati, and she can't fail because My Spirit is with her. Once her reforms are complete, those living in Uttar Pradesh in slave-like conditions will find freedom, justice, security and prosperity. But it will take quite a long time.[98] During that period, you'll learn deep love and compassion for those laboring under the kind of conditions you once created on a lesser scale."

Carson ran from the hall, his head down, shoulders bowed, his whole body reflecting regret at the way he'd lived.[99] He had no glow at all.

Benny turned to Stareweanni once again. "What will happen to Carson?" he asked.

"He'll weep for a time," she said, "and he'll be so heartbroken with soulful remorse that he'll be unable to attend the celebration banquet tonight.[100] But in the coming months Jesus will go to him in person and console him.[101] In time, albeit a long time, Carson will grow to genuinely and deeply love and support those Jesus and Queen Justheart are sending him to live among and learn from."

"Also in time, he'll sincerely rejoice with those who have been honored by the Lord today. He'll be delighted at the great prospects they've been given for impact in this new creation. And he'll find tremendous joy in simply being a part of the perfected Kingdom. He'll also be given opportunities to serve in quiet ways and will discover much satisfaction in those opportunities. You needn't worry for Carson; eventually he will live eternally in the gladness of the Spirit, without bitterness or sorrow."[102]

Despite Stareweanni's comforting words, Benny couldn't help feeling an intense sadness for Carson.

The Reckoning

Chapter 11: Joy

After several other groups came and went, a group that included Tim Crushmann and Ken Songlow was called. Both had been heads of vast ministry efforts, and Benny remembered they had worked together on several projects. It was evident, as they made their way to the stage, that each eagerly hoped to be used by the Lord because of their effective ministry work.

Benny recognized a few others in this band of about forty. The rest of the group appeared to be composed primarily of people who had labored together in the two large ministries, along with their families.

Ken Songlow was the first person up. Benny knew of Ken's work and of how his evangelistic and social outreaches had touched tens of thousands. But Benny knew very little of Ken's early life, so he was intrigued.

Ken's video revealed that, during his first few years after college, he'd developed software for a special-effects firm. He had then opened his own software company, MedImage, in the largest city in Benny's home state. MedImage's products had filled a much-need niche, and the company had done quite well. Ken had eventually branched out into additional areas and had gone international. He had been a significant figure in his state's business community.

Ken's life review included scenes of him using his exceptional wealth to invest heavily in the support of ministries, missions, outreaches, and community development – both at home and overseas. Supporting these efforts became a huge passion for Ken. He certainly enjoyed some of the fruit of his own labor personally, but his heart was in giving it away. And he did so without seeking to control the people or organizations he helped sustain.

Ken also shied away from public recognition for his efforts. His contributions were unsung, and he wanted it that way.

But an event in Ken's early forties thrust him into the public eye ... though that was not his intent. North and South Korea united. The two countries became one, and a huge gateway swung open into the courtyard of north Korean society. With this opening came vast opportunities for the gospel, for social uplift, and for economic investment.

As the clips showed, before this watershed event in Ken's life, he had been an avid follower of affairs in the Koreas. The footage revealed that his grandfather had been a North Korean defector, who had been granted asylum in the United States. It was obvious from the playback that Ken had an abiding love for the culture and people of Korea. He had visited often. He had many relatives in the North and many business associates in the South.

Ken was positioned like few others to help, but the needs and opportunities were far bigger than even Ken's wealth could meet. He needed to enlist the support of others – other entrepreneurs, missionaries, investors, social developers, and technologists. This became his burning passion. And it drove him to get his vision in front of others. Ken founded missional, financial, and social-uplift organizations, and he partnered with other associations as well. He became an able spokesman.

But above all, Ken became a sponsor for evangelism, discipleship, and reconciliation between the peoples of the north and south. In all these endeavors, he let others stand in the spotlight, handling press and media in his stead, whenever possible.

From the onscreen clips, the whole auditorium learned Ken had once been attacked by Northern separatists, former militiamen, who hated his reconciliation efforts. He had sustained permanent injuries. But as he was recovering, he'd made a public appearance forgiving his attackers and asking his partners and supporters to do the same.

Ken lived into his nineties and continued his work to the end. But he did so with reduced mobility and recurrent pain from the assault. Yet it appeared he never allowed it to make him bitter. He was seen telling others, when asked, that he was happy to have given part of his life away to bring life to others; he also said he firmly believed his sacrifice would yield greater service as a bearer of God's image in eternity.[103]

He loved to quote Jim Elliot (a martyred twentieth-century missionary): "He is no fool who gives what he cannot keep to gain what he cannot lose."[104]

When Ken's review was finished, Jesus gave him a broad smile. "Ken," he said, "your life is an example of something that's fairly rare – wealth used well.[105] Your Jim Elliot quote applied as much to your finances as to your body. You've been an exceptionally faithful servant. Because you have sown bountifully, you will reap bountifully."[106]

"I realize you're not a man to seek visibility, preferring instead to stay in the background when possible. Nevertheless, I need people with your genuine spirit as shepherd leaders. You'll be known henceforth as King Forgivingheart. And you'll be a helper king, a shadow shepherd, who is called in as needed to address special circumstances throughout many nations and civilizations."

The audience inhaled collectively, almost a gasp. Was this a quality assignment? Ken's face told them all they needed to know. He was thrilled. "Wow," he said, "I didn't know such a role was possible. You really do know our deepest thoughts, the innermost desires of our souls."

Jesus simply smiled again, stood to his feet, and with a hand gesture caused Ken to glow in soothing crimson splendor. The whole assembly erupted in cheers and whistles.

Chapter 12: Shock

Tim Crushmann was up right behind Ken. He seemed ready for great things. He, and the whole room, had just witnessed Ken's promotion to become King Forgivingheart.

After the standard, and obviously heartfelt, welcome from Jesus, the angels on the large pedestals spread their wings upward and downward, and Tim's story began.

There were clips of his early passion for Jesus in his late teens and young twenties. He told others about Christ's gift of redemption, and he went on mission trips and began speaking in youth gatherings at churches. He then had a stint as a youth pastor for some years.

Next there were scenes of Tim taking a small church in Benny's city. There he began having significant impact in people's lives with effective sermons, with discipleship programs, and with outreach ministries.

But as the church grew, there were also images of Tim becoming impatient and controlling. The first of these incidents occurred when Tim had been the pastor for a little over two years. The church was growing rapidly, but Tim had begun to view the elder board as obstructionist – holding back his big designs for progress. So, in a board meeting, Tim informed the elders he wanted them all to resign or he was going to resign himself. His powerplay worked and they all stepped down. After all, they reasoned aloud to each other, the church was growing like it hadn't in decades, and they were much less essential to that growth than the new pastor. Tim then put elder candidates before the congregation whom he knew wouldn't cross him.

Tim also grew harsh and short with paid team members and sometimes even with volunteers. Eventually, these tyrannical episodes began to dominate Tim's story. He was sometimes downright brutal with staff – yelling at "inadequate" results and firing people without a second thought when they didn't quickly produce the outcomes he wanted. Tim squirmed slightly at these shots, but said nothing.

As the footage continued, the church was still having big impact and growing. The physical plant expanded into a massive campus of several buildings, and Tim's sermons and various ministries were powerful and effective. But behind the curtains were high turnover, high stress, and a dictatorial atmosphere.

Tim was a vigorous man and continued in this vein until he died of a heart attack at 72.

When the playback was complete, Jesus pursed his lips for a moment and then began to speak. "Tim, you had a real passion for me, and in that sense you were an effective servant, producing much fruit. But along the way you became obsessed with impact, with huge results, to the exclusion of almost everything else. You created a churchworld version of 'the end justifies the means.' But *how* is as important to Me as *what*."

"It was never your task to determine how big the harvest should be.[107] Rather it was your job to plant and water diligently.[108] In the end, well-nourished relationships and a gentle spirit are of the greater value than head counts to My everlasting dominion."[109]

"I need leaders in my Kingdom of Kindness who won't run roughshod over others in the name of progress. Throughout human and angelic history, secular leaders have considered people expendable as they sought national, social, or global advancement. But *My* shepherds will bring wholeness without damaging even the most broken or voiceless people, without brushing aside those "little, menial, expendable folk."[110] Instead, My shepherds will take extra care to *elevate* these small ones; they are precious to Me.[111] When I said, 'The gentle will inherit the Earth,' I meant it."[112]

Tim started to protest: "Lord, was it really that serious, given all we accomplished? I mean, I may have been abrupt, but I didn't do any permanent harm, did I?"

One of Tim's longtime staff members, Bren Waters, promptly interjected: "Yes, you did. I feared you then, but no longer. And you seem even now to be blind to your own character."

Jesus drew his breath and started to add to this, but then decided nothing more need be said. This kind of relational accountability was the very reason people were being brought up in small parties that included those closest to them.

Jesus simply continued: "You're being assigned a role living and working among destitute people in the third world who believe there's absolutely nothing special about them, who have no influence in society, and who need to be encouraged and uplifted. You'll be we working under the watchful eye of a shepherd captain known now as Prince Tenderheart. He's a quiet, sensitive man who will help you learn patience and gentleness."[113]

Tim was visibly dissatisfied with the role he'd been given. "Jesus, I imagined I would continue to have great impact like I did before."[114]

"I love you, Tim," Jesus responded, "and you *will* have impact, but it will be still and soft. I simply can't use you as a principal leader with your current heart condition.[115] You had the power of big effects in your first life, but you lacked the heart of a shepherd.[116] It's soul, not bellows and thunder, that will carry My Kingdom in long run. You'll learn to love your silent role in time. And those "little, unimportant" people will become precious to you. I'm giving you a new name, Shepherd Softheart, because that's who you'll become."

With a slow wave of Jesus's hand, Tim's resurrected body began to luminesce, though only lightly, and he made his way toward the upper tiers of the hall.

The outcome of this hearing had been a heavy blow for Tim. But Benny was confident, from Jesus words, that Tim would eventually come to esteem his place in the Kingdom of Kindness.

The Reckoning

Chapter 13: Aftershock

Benny sat contentedly through another few groups, then heard his name called. "Benjamin Little," the archangel cried. Benny's heart skipped a beat, maybe two. It all came down to this – his entire life ... and significant aspects of his eternity as well.

As he moved toward the front, his soul flooded with a mix of emotions. Would it matter that he'd never been much of a leader? Or that he wasn't articulate? Would he even be able to handle it, if he were given some kind of governing responsibility?

As Benny neared the stage, he saw again in Jesus's hands and face the kindness he'd seen in Heaven. And it put him at ease. Whatever happened, Jesus loved him dearly, and he was going to spend eternity in God's Kingdom of Goodness.

As Benny now approached the platform, he was also getting to experience, close up, Jesus's inner council – the senior shepherds surrounding the throne. They too had faces that affirmed the love, care, and gentleness in their hearts. Their warmth, along with Jesus's, was welcoming and uplifting.

Benny's friend Beth, Queen Ferventheart, was now sitting among them. She smiled broadly at Benny and gave him two thumbs up. "You'll do well!" she mouthed.

Joining Benny at the front were several people he'd worked with closely at church. Also in the group were his sister and her earthtime husband, as well as a couple of Benny's coworkers. They all greeted each other as the final few members of the little gang assembled.

Benny tried to keep his mind on each person's story as they were called forward, but he often caught his thoughts wandering to his own life.

At length it was Benny's turn. As he stepped up close enough to touch Jesus, he reached out and Jesus took his hand for just a moment. King Jesus began with the customary greeting. He assured Benny he was a child of God who had an inheritance in this new creation – no matter what the outcome of his examination. Benny had heard the welcome several hundred times already by now. But as Jesus looked directly into his soul with affectionate eyes, Benny sensed down deep that at this moment it was intended for him, and him alone.

The archangels on the two platforms then spread their wings up and down, and Benny's video review started to roll. The opening scene was of his trust in Jesus in college – where his life as a child of God began.[117] Benny immediately recalled that it had taken him some time to become a committed disciple after his spiritual birth. In his twenties, he'd been involved in several promiscuous relationships. Yet none of these showed up in his life's playback. As Benny had grown in spirit, he had eventually ended this behavior. And he'd also sought out the women involved and apologized.

As Benny's chronicle played out on the big screen, very few negative images appeared. Nevertheless, as it advanced, Benny silently remembered numerous times he'd injured someone with hurtful or false words. He had even cheated others on occasion. But he couldn't remember a time when he'd not responded to the Spirit's convicting voice. He'd always sought forgiveness, from both God and the people he'd harmed, and made restitution where appropriate. Benny now knew that these reconciling efforts had removed the incidents from his story.[118]

There was, however, one small series of unfavorable images. In his early adult years, Benny had had a fierce absorption with self which had limited his servanthood. During those years, Benny was consumed, almost entirely, with building a wonderful, pleasure-filled life. As the narrative unfolded, his focus quietly, gradually changed with time. He still enjoyed his favorite comforts and pleasures on occasion, but his passion became helping others. Benny remembered how much joy that peaceful transition had brought him – that slow growth to pouring his life more into others than himself.

As the review proceeded, Benny was surprised to see clips of himself performing his welding and assembly work with enthusiasm and diligence. Until now, Benny hadn't thought much about his job as part of his life message and his servanthood.[119]

There were also images of Benny simply being ready to lend a hand or a dollar wherever the need arose. And there were sequences, as well, of his participation in ministries to aid the sick and the destitute. As Benny aged, these incidents became a larger and larger part of his story.

Benny was a quiet man and not particularly well-spoken. Nevertheless, there were scenes of him sharing his faith or sharing a tidbit of wisdom with others. He'd never been pushy; it wasn't in his personality. But he'd always been attentive and prepared.[120]

Near the midpoint of this visual review, Benny knew the time of his divorce was coming up, and he cringed at the thought of that whole episode showing up on the overhead screen. But much to his surprise, the appropriate spot came and went with no mention of the divorce. Benny was so astonished he asked that the footage be paused.

"Jesus, wasn't my divorce a huge spiritual failure? Yet the video has skipped it completely. Can you help me understand that?"

"Benny, your divorce *was* a great spiritual failure. But single failures or sins, even big ones, don't define your servanthood.[121] In the years after your divorce, you did all you could to bring harmony, reconciliation, and even restitution."

"King David was a murderer and adulterer who repented and made his sin an isolated incident. ... And he sits right there," Jesus said, as He pointed to one of the shining figures surrounding the throne. David smiled softly and nodded subtly.

Jesus resumed: "As we recreate this beautiful Kingdom, David will reign over the nation Israel.[122] Real servanthood is about the central course of your life, not about single points of failure.[123] It's true that longstanding patterns of sin can damage your walk so dramatically that stewardship becomes blighted or ineffective. But that wasn't the case with you. That's why your whole divorce episode is not part of your story ... just as David's sin was no longer part of his story, when he stood exactly where you're standing some weeks ago."

Benny nodded to show he was getting it.

As Benny's playback moved into the second half, it included scenes of sacrifice and suffering because of his faith. Benny was so concerned for the broken and impoverished he'd sometimes overlooked his own needs or desires to meet theirs. Instead of actually buying a three-wheeler, Benny was content simply to admire them on display ... in order to help more.

And he'd labored physically to meet others' needs, participating in mission trips to help build wells and windmills for desperate farmers in arid countries. The farmers appreciated his work to uplift their lives, yet sometimes had no desire for his *spiritual* wealth. He kept serving them anyway.

At home, Benny was occasionally ridiculed for his faith, especially for his depth of commitment. He was chided for his "excessive" involvement in his church community and for the "old-fashioned" standards of morality to which he held himself. He was also rebuffed for his consuming focus on spiritual matters and for his "overgiving" – of money, but especially of time – which deprived him, in the eyes of others, of some of life's biggest luxuries and greatest pleasures.

Benny had also at times suffered things that felt more like real persecution. He was fired from a midcareer position after being promoted to supervisor ... because he had reported an illegal substitution of manufacturing materials when he'd discovered it.

Benny had even been ousted from a community charity focused on social justice; they discovered he was actively participating in a program that challenged men to be spiritual leaders in their homes. The program denigrated women, they said; it implied they shouldn't be spiritual leaders.

Through it all, Benny had remained positive and committed. One sequence showed Benny describing to a friend how he had taken to heart Jesus's words about the treasures of heaven that were to be awarded at Christ's throne.[124] It was evident that Benny had embraced Jesus's admonition to give our lives away now in order to receive the fullest of lives in eternity.[125] Benny explained to the friend that he had come to realize something: his mortal life was, in large part, a training ground. And anything he sacrificed or suffered because of his discipleship was insignificant compared to the heart-wealth he stood to gain in exchange in Christ's coming Kingdom.[126]

When his life's chronicle was complete, Benny was generally pleased with the unified story he felt it told. And it seemed Jesus was pleased too.

"Benny," He said, "you weren't a big mover or shaker, but you were profoundly faithful with the talent and treasure you were given. You have served extremely well."

After a dramatic pause, Jesus continued: "You'll be joining the men and women sitting around me, and you'll be known as King Trueheart!"[127]

Benny's whole body tensed. "Lord Jesus," he replied weakly, "I'm very moved and honored, but I have no leadership skills. How can I be qualified to serve in such a prominent role?"

Jesus laughed warmly. "Benny, have I mentioned today that serving in My reign is far more about heart than skill or achievement?[128] It's your *heart* that I want and need to help build and sustain My Kingdom. I will be with you in this; my Spirit will be upon you; you cannot fail. I'll also assign aids, governors, and undershepherds who will help carry out the wisdom of your heart in effective, impactful ways. You needn't be apprehensive at all."

Benny let out a soft sigh, and small tears of joy welled up in his eyes. He was a little ashamed of how emotional he was. But Jesus assured him it was okay: "This is a big and unexpected day for you, Benny. You'll serve *with* Me and *for* Me in an unusually close way, forever. Forever, My dear friend. That's a long time. You needn't be ashamed of the emotion that brings."

With a wave of Jesus's hand, Benny began to shine as brightly as those already seated around the throne. An angel pointed Benny to an empty chair among the dazzling ones. As Benny approached it, he realized it was a modest mini-throne. And the chair had his new name already engraved in the top, "King Trueheart."

Benny could hear the throng of angels and humans roar as Jesus said, "Let's hear it for King Trueheart, my faithful servant."

But the noise of the crowd was quite muted, very recessive, in Benny's thoughts as the words of King Jesus rang loudly and repeatedly in his in soul: "You were profoundly faithful.... You have served extremely well.... You'll serve *with* Me and *for* Me in an unusually close way, forever."

Chapter 14: Afterglow

As Benny reentered the Great Hall for the evening's activity, he noticed how striking its open ceiling was under the night sky. The moon and stars provided soft, low light – which was gracefully amplified and diffused by the crystalline mist of the vapor canopy high above.

Unlike the scene earlier, during his daylong participation in the Judgment Seat proceedings, all those in the hall were already glowing. He realized that the children of God who'd failed to take on any luminescence were not at the banquet.

He asked one of the attending angels about their absence and was informed that those who had given off no light during their mortal lives were too filled with regret to attend.[129] Most were quietly weeping in contrition and remorse in the sprawling, tree-filled, and now-darkened gardens surrounding the Great Hall.[130] Benny knew there were hundreds of places in that vast park for solitude and private reflection.

The angel said these unlit ones were contemplating both their misspent lives and the austere, reformational assignments that lay ahead of them.[131] The angel assured

Benny that in time (just as Stareweanni had said of his friend Carson) their sorrow would turn to joy. They would come to savor the eternal Kingdom of Light they were to be a part of. And they would be glad for the roles their faithful comrades had been given to shape eternity. In short, they would learn to rejoice with those who rejoice, to live beyond themselves, and to love deeply.

In the middle of the Great Hall was a huge round table. Throughout the rest of the chamber were many smaller tables, also round. The comfortable stadium-style seats, which were used by the audience earlier in the day, had been removed. And the chamber was festively decorated in a Spring harvest motif. The garnishments included bright floral accents all around.

A pleasant aroma in the grand hall matched the decor; the whole place smelled soothingly of fresh grain and baked bread.

Excited chatter filled the air. But it was not muted as before, when Benny had entered the hall for the morning tribunal. Instead, it was lively, almost boisterous.

The usher angel to whom Benny had already spoken pointed him to his seat at the large, central table. Benny arrived there to find his new name, "King Trueheart," engraved on a small, smooth, white stone marking his place.[132] Benny ran his fingers lightly over the stone, feeling the contrast between the polished surface and the inscribed letters.

Apart from the plants that created the Spring motif, everything set for the banquet was white – from the namestones to the curved granite chairs and the tablecloths and napkins. Even the utensils were white, made of some kind of dense porcelain.

Benny realized the hall, in this configuration, seated far fewer people than it had earlier in the day.[133] But he also remembered that a large number of people, more than he could count, had had nothing to offer Jesus in their stories. They had been given no afterglow and had run from the tribunal in anguish, mortified at their own wasted lives.[134] Benny couldn't help feeling a twinge of sorrow for them once again. But he knew Jesus had given them every opportunity, through the labor of His Holy Spirit, to live well for God. And he knew their mourning was only temporary. He quickly returned to the joy of the grand celebration that was about to commence.

Benny realized he was seated right next to Jesus at the table – because, at the place adjacent to Benny's, lay a white stone, much larger than his, engraved "King of Kings." On the opposite side of the King of Kings' seat was a stone engraved "Queen Ferventheart," Benny's missionary friend.

Next to Benny, on the side away from Jesus's place, was a stone bearing the name "King Forgivingheart." He recognized this as the new name of Ken Songlow, the generous sponsor of Korean reconciliation and outreach that Jesus had appointed to kingship earlier in the day.

Only these three, Ferventheart, Trueheart, and Forgivingheart, had been inducted into the ranks of full royal shepherdship on this appraisal day.

The remainder of the seats at the central table bore the names of those who had been appointed as viceshepherds, as regional governors, or as judges of angelic civilizations. Some of these shepherds were already seated in their places, and Benny was fascinated at how different in color and glint each person's bodyglow was.

It wasn't long before Queen Ferventheart entered and found her place on the other side of Jesus's chair. Her earthtime husband took his seat directly across the table from Bethany, and he was all smiles – just delighted to have such a significant a part to play in Jesus's grand eternal mission.

The gala room was nearly full now, with luminescent bodies everywhere. At a nearby table Benny noticed Mea, the former ministry head of The Heart's Home. She too was smiling broadly, cherishing her place in Christ's restorative mission and eternal reign.

As the time for the celebration arrived, a set of six angels, two at either end of the hall and a pair in the middle, blew great trumpets. These horns broadcast a much lighter, more melodic feel than the solemn horns used earlier in the day. Everyone stood ... and Jesus entered the Great Hall, which was now transformed into a magnificent banquet room. As Jesus made His way to the center, He stopped at almost every table and greeted at least a couple of people at each one.

Benny noted Jesus pausing to give Tim Crushmann, the pastor who had been so domineering in his first life, a warm hug. Tim clearly appreciated it, though it seemed to Benny that Tim wasn't entirely past the shock of the day's earlier events. But Benny was sure Tim, with time and growth,[135] would move to a new state of joy and adore his place in the Great Kingdom.

Once Jesus had taken his seat, everyone else sat down as well. Angels then came and poured drinks for all.[136]

Next, Jesus stood up and addressed the whole assembly: "This night is a celebration – a celebration of My return to Earth, but also a celebration of your faithfulness, love, and work on My behalf.[137] Enjoy the evening and all these friends. We'll have many more festive occasions, but remember this as we rejoice: we still have much work to do."

"We must restore the spheres of humans and angels to the harmony, uprightness, and abundance Our Father intended when he first asked Me to create the cosmos.[138] And we must bring all His enemies into complete submission to Him.[139] Those enemies include spiritual darkness, deprivation, injustice, oppression, and violent conflict – along with all the power structures that foster them. Each of you will be anointed by My angels later this evening to empower you for this task of restoration."

"I, as the Implementor of the Father's Eternal Plan, have already begun a restoration of the natural creation. Our atmosphere is now storm-free, and fresh water is becoming abundant everywhere. New plants will soon be developed under the care of those of you who have gardening assignments. And this new vegetation will make food plentiful everywhere. It will also satisfy even the most extreme carnivores.[140] The hardy food supply, together with the guiding help of the animal shepherds among us, will bring all wildlife on our Earth into equilibrium and harmony."[141]

"Then it will be up to the rest of us, those whose roles are primarily among humans and angels, to do the balance of the work. Just as the curse fell on the world gradually, so it will (with our help) be lifted from the world gradually."[142]

"We must bring everyone together in unity and peace. We must implement compassion and justice. We must create new canals and farms and prosperous, clean cites where no one is left behind. And we must ensure all living things – from the tiniest furry creature to the most majestic angel – are treated with kindness, attention, and care."

"When we have completed our restorative task, aided by the Spirit's revitalizing work, God Himself will come to live with us here.[143] Our current Jerusalem, Ariel, will become the *New Jerusalem*. And Heaven and Earth will quite literally be one – in both location and spirit. This city will be the absolute center of government for the entire universe."

"Tonight, rejoice; celebrate what we have begun!"

As Jesus sat down, the whole assembly, Benny included, thundered joyfully ... cheering the noble King Jesus and his eternal enterprise. They hailed their Redeemer and the vast assignment and opportunity He had given them.

Like earlier in the day, the noise receded rapidly in Benny's head as Jesus's fresh words resounded over and over in his mind. Benny couldn't wait to get started with their mission. But he didn't allow himself to get lost in thought for long. After all, he was sitting next to Jesus, the King of Kings, the Wonderful Counselor,[144] and he wasn't going to lose a minute of it.

The Reckoning

Epilogue

This short story was intended to fire your imagination as a way of getting you to think seriously about your life beyond *this* life. The Judgment Seat of Christ is a central event in the future of every believer. It's an event that will impact you forever. And forever is a very long time.

We do well not to lose sight of eternity. Jesus expects us to be driven by an awareness of it (Mat 6:1, 19:21; Luke 6:22-23, 12:32-34, 16:9-11; 2 Cor 4:17; James 1:12; Rev 2:17, 2:26-27, 3:12, 3:21). And He asks us to give our lives away now to receive a much richer life then (Luke 12:32-34, John 12:25-26,[145] Mat 16:24-27, Mark 8:34-38, Luke 14:12-14).

There's a twist, however. That rich life meets God's definition of everlasting richness, not ours. Eternal wealth is the opportunity to live in the fulness of our identities as God's image – *forever*. It means receiving the authority to shine forth as unleashed emitters of God's glory. It means possessing the power and mandate to positively shape every corner of the cosmos as His mature, trusted sons and daughters. It means living as His anointed shepherds of creation.

If you'd like to know more about eternity and about how to be prepared for the Judgment Seat of Christ, please take advantage of the following resources:

Life Beyond Heaven: Where You Can Make Your Biggest Impact on Earth, Dan Lee (WordForge Press, 2018)

Heaven, Randy Alcorn (Tyndale House Publishers, 2004)

Your Eternal Reward: Triumph and Tears at the Judgment Seat of Christ, Erwin Lutzer (Moody Press, 1998)

If you believe the message of this book will be valuable to others, please consider writing a brief review on Amazon.

Where Did He Get That?
Notes on Biblical Sources

---

[1] The author's book *Life Beyond Heaven: where you can make your biggest impact on Earth* describes eternity in detail. Distinct from many books about heaven and eternity, *Life Beyond Heaven* is based on an examination of the entire range of biblical texts dealing with the subject – from both the Old and New Testaments – rather than on a handful of verses in Revelation.

[2] This assumes that, when Jesus renews the physical creation (Rev 21:5, Acts 3:21 Mat 19:28 {NRSV}), the water vapor canopy of Gen 1:7 and 7:11 is also restored.

[3] Mat 17:2, Rev 1:16

[4] Mat 28:2-3

[5] Dan 12:3, Mat 13:43. 1 Cor 15:40-42 implies there will be differences in radiance.

[6] 1 Cor 15:40-41 – just as "star differs from star in shining forth."

[7] The idea that time does not exist in Heaven or in eternity is a popular one, but is completely unsupported by scripture. Rev 8:1, 22:1-2; Zech 14:8-9 with 16.

[8] Sleep is the New Testament description of physical death for the child of God – Mat 27:52, John 11:11-13, 1 Thes 4:14.

[9] Luke 23:43, 2 Cor 12:4

[10] Heb 12:22-24, Rev 20:4

[11] 1 Chr 16:31, Psa 89:6 (AMPC), Isa 1:2, Isa 24:21 (NIV)

---

[12] Isa 24:21 (NIV, LB). The identification of the angels with the stars is strong in scripture, so strong they are sometimes used interchangeably (e.g., Job 38:7 {NIV}, Isa 14:13-14 {NIV}) ... just as "Earth" and "humankind" are often used interchangeably in scripture (e.g., Gen 11:1 {NRSV}).

[13] 1 Cor 15:35-54

[14] 2 Cor 5:1-4

[15] 1 Cor 15:52

[16] 1 Thes 4:16-17

[17] 2 Cor 5:1-4

[18] Isa 29:7-8

[19] Rev 21:2-3, 10-11; 3:12

[20] Heb 12:22 with 9:11 and 11:10

[21] Rev 21:10-17. This passage is technically a description of the New Jerusalem, that is, Heaven come down to Earth out of the heavens when God the Father comes to dwell here. But it is reasonable to assume that the restored Jerusalem of Christ's initial return will be its precursor in many respects. See Mic 4:1; Jer 3:17, 31:38-40; and Zech 2:3-11 (where "Me" in verses 8, 9, and 11 is almost certainly Jesus, the Messiah).

[22] Rev 21:1

[23] ~ Seas are taken up – Rev 21:1, Isa 51:9-11.
  ~ The Apocalypse is described in Mat 24:6-31; Joel 3:9-18; Isa 33:3-14; Zeph 1:2-18, 3:8; Rev 6:1-12, 8:1-9:20.

[24] The Holy Spirit is also the Spirit of Christ, doing the creative work of Christ - 1 Pet 1:11, Col 1:15-16. The Spirit is the force of creation – Gen 1:2. The water vapor canopy of Gen 1:7 and 7:11 is

---

presumably restored when Jesus renews the physical creation –
Rev 21:5, Acts 3:21, Mat 19:28 (NRSV).

25 Gen 1:6-7, 7:11; Acts 3:21

26 Isa 11:6-9, 65:25

27 Isa 11:6-9

28 2 Cor 5:10, Rom 14:10 {NKJV}

29 John 12:26; Rev 2:10, 26; Rom 2:10

30 Luke 20:33-36

31 Rev 8:2

32 1 King 6:27, 2 Chr 3:11

33 Heb 1:7

34 1 Cor 13:1

35 Isa 29:7-8; "Ariel" means "lion of God" in Hebrew.

36 Rev 21:2-3, 23-24

37 Heb 2:10 (NKJV)

38 Rev 19:7, 21:2; Dan 7:27 (NRSV), 2 Tim 2:12 (TPT)

39 Isa 42:1-4, Rom 8:19, Rev 2:26-27 (HCSB – in verse 27,
"shepherd" is a more accurate translation than "rule.")

40 Rev 21:2-3

41 Rev 21:2-3: Zech 2:10, 8:3; Joel 3:17; Gen 3:8; Isa 24:13-15,
51:3-4

42 Rev 2:26, 2 Tim 2:12 (TPT)

43 Col 1:12, 1 Thes 5:4-5, 1 Pet 2:9, Jam 1:17

44 Rev 22:12; Heb 10:32-37; Luke 14:13-14, 16:10, 6:35 (where
"you will be sons," is best translated "mature children" – Greek

huios); Mat 5:11-12; Gal 6:8-10 (where "eternal life" is not a reference to salvation, but to "the absolute fullness of life" in eternity – Thayer's Greek Lexicon); 2 Cor 9:6

[45] ~ Jesus as Shepherd and King: Heb 13:20 with 1 Tim 6:15.
   ~ Jesus as Creator: Col 1:15-16.
   ~ Believers as Christ's companions – Heb 1:9
   ~ Believers as co-shepherds with Jesus: 2 Tim 2:12 (TPT); Jer 3:15-17; Rev 2:26-28 (HSCB – "shepherd" is a more literal translation than "rule" in verse 27.)

[46] Dan 12:3; 1 Pet 2:9 (NLT) (We are designed to "show forth" his character both now and in eternity.)

[47] Jer 3:15-17, Rev 2:26-27 (HCSB – "shepherd" is a more literal translation than "rule" in verse 27, as every major lexical work attests), Psa 78:70-72 with 1 Sam 16:7, Mat 5:5

[48] Gen 1:26-28, Jer 23:3-5, Heb 2:5-8

[49] Eph 6:12, Isa 24:21 (LB): "On that day the Lord will punish the fallen angels in the heavens and the proud rulers of the nations on earth."

[50] 1 Cor 6:3 (ISV)

[51] Rev 20:7, 11-15

[52] Mat 13:43, Dan 12:3

[53] Dan 12:3, Mat 13:43, 1 Cor 15:40-42 with 2 Cor 9:6

[54] Rev 3:12 where "pillars" are pillars of the New Jerusalem community and the temple is the throne room of God and Christ (Heb 4:14-16).

[55] When Christ returns, there is still much that is broken, desperate, and amiss in the world. The restoration of God's

creation will take time – Psa 72:11-12; Isa 42:1-4; Mic 4:1-6, 5:4-6; Psa 2:6-12; 1 Cor 15:25-28.

[56] That some believers will receive remedial character building is taught in several places in scripture - notably Mal 3:1-3 with 1 Cor 3:13-15, 2 Cor 5:10-11, Mat 18:21-35, Col 3:23-25, Luke 12:43 (representing Christ's return) with 47-48.

[57] This is a mistaken application of Mat 22:30. Those angels who are now in Heaven are no longer involved in marriage or procreation. (The same will be true of humankind.) But angels did once marry and have sex – Gen 6:1-4. Note that in Gen 6 the term "sons of God" (Hebrew *ben elohiym*) is almost certainly a reference to angels. The term is translated "heavenly beings" in some versions. There is no controversy that this is the meaning of the term elsewhere in the Old Testament, and this is way the ancients understood the term in Gen 6.

[58] Gen 6:1-4, Jude 1:6. Angelic sexuality, like human sexuality, was misused by some. Many millennia ago, a lustful band of angels received severe discipline from God for abusing the gift of sexuality and mating with human women. In Gen 6, "sons of God" (Hebrew *ben elohiym*) is almost certainly a reference to angels, and it is translated "heavenly beings," in some versions. Jude 1:6 makes little sense if it is not referring to Gen 6:1-4.

[59] Luke 20:34-35

[60] Col 1:11-14

[61] Mic 4:1-2

[62] Mat 5:44-48

[63] Luke 19:12-27; 1 Cor 4:2

[64] Isa 1:17, Luke 14:12-14, Rev 3:17-19

[65] Mat 28:19-20; Luke 14:33, 16:9-11

[66] Luke 12:48b: "To whom much is given, of him is much required."

[67] Mat 6:19-21, Luke 12:33-34

[68] 2 Cor 9:6

[69] When Christ returns, there is still much that is in need of redemption – 1 Cor 15:25-28; Psa 72:11-12; Isa 42:1-4; Mic 4:1-6, 5:4-6; Psa 2:6-12.

[70] Mat 24:6-31; Joel 3:9-18; Isa 33:3-14; Zeph 1:2-18, 3:8; Rev 6:1-12, 8:1-9:20

[71] Heb 12:17; Luke 19:12-27; Rev 3:11, 17-18

[72] Jer 3:15, 1 Sam 16:7 with Psa 78:70-72

[73] Mat 6:1-6

[74] 1 Cor 3:6-9, Mat 13:23

[75] Mat 25:21

[76] Acts 7:55

[77] Compare Elijah's commendation by God, despite his sullenness – 1 Kings 19:4, 10, and 14 with 2 Kings 2:11-12

[78] Luke 16:10

[79] Luke 14:8-9, John 12:26

[80] Luke 19:41-44

[81] Mat 11:28-30

[82] Rom 2:4

[83] Mat 5:13-16

[84] Isa 6:5, Dan 9:20, Jer 8:18-22

[85] 1 Cor 13:1-2

[86] In keeping with Mat 7:1-2

[87] Mat 5:24-26

[88] Luke 12:3

[89] 1 John 2:28, Mark 8:38

[90] "If we are unfaithful, he remains faithful, since he cannot deny himself" (2 Tim 2:13 {NET}). As believers we are now in Him, part of Him.

[91] 2 Cor 5:17

[92] Rom 8:10 (RSV), 1 Pet 3:18 (RSV)

[93] Like the servants who were given the opportunity to invest their talents (Mat 25:14-30, NIV), our new birth provides a potentiality, a capacity given to us by the Master that did not previously exist. But what we do with that is entirely up to us. We can still let sin completely rule our existence (Rom 6:12). We can utterly forsake communion with the Source of our new being (1 John 2:28). And we can fail to "put on the new self" implied by our new being (Eph 4:21-24). These warnings and commands: 1) to "not let sin reign," 2) to "abide in Him," 3) to "put on the new self," are meaningless, if it were not possible to Christians to refuse to do so. But the consequence is not the loss of salvation – otherwise the "free gift" is no longer free (Rom 5:15-18, 6:23, NRSV) and is, instead, dependent on our deeds or works – a clear contradiction of scripture (Eph 2:8-9; Rom 3:28, 4:6; Gal 2:16).

[94] Luke 19:12-27. See also 2 Tim 2:12: "If we are joined with him in his sufferings, then we will reign together with him in his triumph. But if we disregard him, then he will also disregard us" (TPT).

[95] When Christ returns, there is still much that is broken, desperate, and amiss in the world. The restoration of God's

creation will take time – Psa 72:11-12; Isa 42:1-4; Mic 4:1-6, 5:4-6; Psa 2:6-12; 1 Cor 15:25-28.

[96] While the events of the Apocalypse will significantly reduce the earth's population, scripture in no way suggests the Earth will suddenly be rid of evil as a result (Psa 72:11-12; Isa 42:1-4; Mic 4:1-6, 5:4-6; Psa 2:6-12; 1 Cor 15:25-28). Even as this book (*The Reckoning)* is being written, an estimated 8 million people live in slavery in India (Global Slavery Index). This figure is based on conservative, cold-eyed definition of slavery. For example, "forced marriage" includes sale of girls into forced marriages, but not traditional arranged marriages. (globalslaveryindex.org/2018/findings/country-studies/india/).

[97] 1 Cor 3:15, Heb 4:9-11, Luke 12:47, Mal 3:1-3

[98] Isa 42:1-4 with Rev 2:26-27 (HCSB), 1 Cor 15:25-28 with 2 Tim 2:12 (TPT)

[99] 1 John 2:28

[100] Jam 4:8-9, Ecc 3:1-4 – this is a time to weep. Mat 25:14-30 specifically describes weeping at Christ's return when he judges his servants. In Mat 25, the "unprofitable servant" (NKJV) is still a servant, not an unbeliever; see Luke 19:12-27 parallel (especially verses 21-27). The NIV translation of Mat 25:30, "outside, into the darkness," is an accurate rendering of the Greek. In the tradition of first-century Judeans, a household would celebrate the master's return with an evening banquet. In the parable, the unfaithful servant does not participate, but weeps outside. I understand it to be the unfaithful servant's own shame and remorse (weeping and gnashing of teeth) that bind him and keep him from attending the banquet.

[101] Isa 25:8, Rev 7:17

[102] Rom 14:17

[103] John 12:25-26 (where "eternal life" is not a reference to salvation, but to "the absolute fullness of life" in eternity – Thayer's Greek Lexicon), 2 Cor 4:17, Rom 8:17-18. As many commentators have pointed out, in Rom 8:17, being an heir of God is the reality of every child of God, but being a coheir with Christ, the Firstborn Son, is contingent on "suffering with Him, that we may be glorified with Him." Persevering and standing firm in the face of hardship leads to sharing in Christ's shining forth with God's character and good dominion, "His glory," in eternity.

[104] From Elliot's journal entry for Oct 28,1949. Elliot refers to Luke 16:9 in the same entry. This citation of Elliot has been updated slightly with more modern language: Elliot's "that which he cannot" has been replaced with "what he cannot."

[105] Mat 19:24 and Mar 10:25, where "enter the Kingdom of God" is probably better translated "share in the reign of God." See also 1 Cor 1:26-27 and Luke 6:24-25. In Luke 6, Jesus give a dire warning to the wealthy because of the attitude that was common among them in His day – namely, self-absorption, obsession with a life of pleasure and luxury.

[106] 2 Cor 9:6

[107] 1 Cor 3:7

[108] 1 Cor 3:6-7

[109] 1 Cor 13:2, 1 Sam 16:7, Mat 5:5

[110] Isa 42:1-4 – "He will not break a bruised reed or put out a weakly burning candle." Even the most shattered and powerless in society will not be disregarded or brushed out of the way.

[111] Jer 23:4 with Psa 72:11-14

[112] Mat 5:5

---

[113] This follows the spirit of Luke 12:42-46. The abusive lead servant is "cut in pieces," an idiom for a harsh scolding, equivalent to "tear you to shreds." He is then assigned with the other "unfaithful" (NRSV) for reformation. "The unfaithful" is also translated "the disloyal" (CJB) and "the servants who cannot be trusted" (CEB). MSG captures the sense well: "The master will ... give him the thrashing of his life, and put him back in the kitchen peeling potatoes."

[114] Mat 19:30

[115] We sometimes imagine we'll fall asleep an untrustworthy servant and awaken a trusted one. But scripture doesn't support that idea. There is otherwise no need for the refiner's fire after the Judgment Seat of Christ – 1 Cor 3:15 with Mal 3:1-3, 2 Cor 5:10-11, Mat 18:21-35, Col 3:23-25, Luke 12:43 (representing Christ's return) with 47-48.

[116] Ps 78:70-72 with 1 Sam 16:7

[117] John 1:12, Rom 8:10 (RSV)

[118] Mat 5:24-25, Rom 12:18

[119] Col 3:22-24

[120] 1 Pet 3:15

[121] Compare Mat 26:73-75 with John 21:14-17 and Luke 22:28-30

[122] Jer 30:8-10; Ezek 34:22-24, 37:22-25, Hosea 3:4-5. Note that the twelve apostles will apparently rule the individual tribes under David's national authority (Mat 19:28, Luk 22:28-30).

[123] 1 Cor 3:13-15. The worthless is burned up, and it is what remains that matters. Of course, if our entire life is about building the worthless, nothing will remain.

[124] 2 Cor 5:10; Mat 5:10-12, 10:39-42: Luke 14:13-14; Mark 10:21

---

[125] Mat 16:24-25, Luke 16:9-12

[126] 2 Cor 4:17, 2 Tim 2:12 (TPT)

[127] Mat 19:30

[128] Isa 66:2, 1 Sam 61:7 with Psa 78:70-72, Rev 2:26-27 (HCSB – "shepherd" is a more literal translation than "rule" in verse 27.)

[129] 1 John 2:28, Luke 9:26

[130] Jam 4:8-9, Ecc 3:1-4 – this is a time to weep. Mat 25:14-30 specifically describes weeping at Christ's return when he judges his servants. In Mat 25, the "unprofitable servant" (verse 30, NRSV) is still a servant, not an unbeliever; see Luke 19:12-27 (particularly the contrast in verse 21-27 between the unproductive servant and the unbeliever). The NIV translation of Mat 25:30, "outside, into the darkness," is an accurate rendering of the Greek. In the tradition of first-century Judea, a household would celebrate the master's return with an evening banquet. In the parable, the unfaithful servant does not participate, but weeps outside in the dark. I understand it to be the unfaithful servant's own shame and remorse (weeping and gnashing of teeth) that bind him and keep him from attending the banquet.

[131] That some believers will receive remedial character building is taught in several places in scripture - notably Mal 3:1-3 with 1 Cor 3:13-15, 2 Cor 5:10-11, Mat 18:21-35, Col 3:23-25, Luke 12:43 (representing Christ's return) with 47-48.

[132] Rev 2:17. The narrative speculates that on one side of the stone is a public name, while on the backside is an intimate, affectionate name.

[133] Mat 22:14. Many (all believers) are called to be Christ's eternal shepherds, but few are chosen.

[134] 1 John 2:28

---

135 The popular notion that there is no growth in eternity is not supported by scripture – Mic 4:1-2, Mal 3:1-3 with 1 Cor 3:13-15, Rev 14:3. As Mal 3 and 1 Cor 3 imply, some of that growth is clearly remedial. While the old sin nature (the flesh) is gone, the impression it has made on our souls (especially in the form of any remaining false values and false beliefs about ourselves) will be removed as a *process* of purification. This process will ultimately be complete before God the Father comes to dwell on earth – i.e., the *second* phase of eternity.

136 Heb 1:13-14

137 Luke 22:28-30, Rev 19:6-9, Mark 14:25

138 John 1:1-3

139 1 Cor 15:24-28 with Rev 2:26-27 (HCSB). Note that ESV captures the second half of the phrase accurately: and they will shepherd them with a rod of iron, "*as when earthen pots are broken in pieces.*" It is not people, but power structures, that are shattered.

140 Isa 11:7, 65:25

141 Isa 11:6-9

142 Both Rev 22:1-4 and Zech 14:9-11 declare that the curse will be lifted entirely as the restorative phase of eternity is completed. But that lifting will be a process (1 Cor 15:25-28, Isa 42:1-4), just as falling under the curse was a process. For example, though the curse was declared against Adam and Eve (Gen 2:17, 3:16-19), humans still lived to ages approaching 1,000 years until the time of Noah (Gen 5:1-27). And even after Noah, ages fell only gradually to reach today's typical lifespan of about 80 years (Ps 90:10). Noah lived 950 years (Gen 9:29), his son, Shem, 600 years (Gen 11:10-11), Eber, Shem's great grandson, 464 (Gen 16:16-17), Isaac 180 (Gen 35:28), Joseph 110 (Gen 50:26).

[143] Rev 21:2-3, 22:1-4

[144] Isa 9:6

[145] In verse 25, "eternal life" is not a reference to salvation, but to "the absolute fullness of life" in eternity – Thayer's Greek Lexicon.

The Reckoning

Abbreviations of Bible Translations

AMPC	The Amplified Bible – Classic Edition
CEB	Common English Bible
CJB	Complete Jewish Bible
ESV	English Standard Version
HCSB	Holman Standard Christian Bible
ISV	International Standard Version
MSG	The Message
LB	The Living Bible
NET	New English Translation
NIV	New International Version
NKJV	New King James Version
NRSV	New Revised Standard Version
RSV	Revised Standard Version
TPT	The Passion Translation

About the Author

DAN LEE was not a guy you'd have predicted would write a sobering, frontrow account of the Judgment Seat of Christ. During his undergrad years he loved nerdy, fantasy and sci fi stuff, and his hero was the emotionless Mr. Spock from Star Trek. (Seriously? How did he ever find a wife?)

Dan had trouble deciding what he wanted to be when he grew up and spent his first few years out of college as a big-city cop. But he didn't really have the gritty temperament for it and accepted a commission in the U.S. Navy – ultimately rising to the rank of Commander. He eventually moved to the private sector, where he led defense technology studies.

Dan had a spiritual awakening around age forty ... in which he discovered the *real* eternity (the biblical eternity – a dynamic, exhilarating place). And he saw the impact of the Judgment Seat of Christ on our individual roles there. He's been helping churches ever since (from megachurches to house churches) energize their members with eternity's motivating power.

After completing a joint PhD-ThD in religious studies and theology in 2015, he retired early from the private sector to devote more time to the message of our incomparable eternal future and the call to action it fosters.

Dan has discovered the great entertainment value of grandkids, thanks to his three daughters. He also loves chocolate, documentaries, biking, and watching deer out his back window. He lives near Weatherford, Texas with his wife, Betsi.

dan@drdanlee.com

www.ingramcontent.com/pod-product-compliance
Lightning Source LLC
Chambersburg PA
CBHW020618130626
46552CB00003B/1021